When They Bully: Rainbow Girl

By Regina Smith

Disclaimer

Copyright 2020 © by Regina Smith

All Rights Reserved

Cover design and Photography by Elena Dudina

For Ken and Lillie

Chapter 1

Now in the twelfth grade, Kendra Williams waited patiently for the bell to ring at Wood Oak High School. Her family had deep roots in Wood Oak, Louisiana going back several generations. She wanted to be the first in her family to move away to another state after she would graduate from high school; yet, she still had one more year to finish. Determined, she wanted to make sure that she made the best grades possible for her to be able to get a scholarship to a good university. Her parents worked two jobs each to make sure that she had a secure future although they both still struggled financially due to recent car payments. Mrs. Williams' car recently stopped working, forcing the family to need an additional car. Luckily, they were able to get a new one with payments so that transportation was no longer an issue. However, since the family lived a block away from the school, Kendra did not have to worry about having a vehicle because she was able to walk to and from school.

As soon as the bell rang, Kendra walked to her locker to gather her books for the day. She mainly took honors courses, except for her electives which included both her art and gym classes. She enjoyed those classes the most but was beginning to have problems in her other classes. There were three girls that had taken the initiative to make her life miserable: Whitney Foster, Jarika Knowles, and Dominique Greene. For some odd reason, there was a common link between them, and a boy named James Boudreaux. It seemed that all three girls would give her a hard time whenever he would try to associate with her, no matter how small the interactions would be. While she ignored their rude comments towards her, things only got worse once James had switched into her art class and sat directly next to her. He wasn't rude or disrespectful to Kendra. He just sat down next to her smiling, somewhat mesmerized. Often, he would ignore the instructions from the teacher, Ms. Montrell, and try to sneak glances at Kendra, almost to the point of adding more to her already overwhelming insecurities.

"Why is he always staring at me?" Kendra thought. "I hope he isn't looking because of the rumors of what people are saying. I'm so tired of being judged by everyone."

Even though he was now sitting next to her, neither of them had any direct words exchanged between them until the day before when he had announced that he was going to be in the art club and transferred into the art class. Additionally, he was still no stranger to her even before then, he had been in her family's life long ago when he was best friends with her twin brother, Cecil, who died years ago. Her twin brother, Cecil Williams, who had long been deceased many years ago was best friends with James. When both Cecil and Kendra were in the first grade, he would come home daily talking about James and how he enjoyed his company.

"I'd like to meet this James person you are speaking about," Mrs. Williams said years ago. *"Maybe you can invite him to your birthday since it is coming up real soon."*

"I'm sure he will come, he is my best friend," said Cecil smiling. *"He likes the same things that I*

like such as, "Captain Sun" and we play it every day at recess."

Once the day came for the birthday party to happen, Cecil waited anxiously for James to arrive. Most of the other kids from school had already arrived and were playing the games with most of the adults.

"Why are you still waiting by the door?" Kendra asked Cecil, taking a bite out of a cupcake.

"I'm waiting on James," said Cecil. "He is going to show up! I just know it!"

"Well, why don't you go and play with the other kids," said Mrs. Williams. "Once James arrives, I will let you know. What does he look like, dear?"

"He has black hair and blue eyes," Cecil said. "He is a little shorter than me and he is loud like me!"

"If he is loud like you, I am sure we will hear him before we see him," Mrs. Williams laughed. "Now, go and play with the other kids and I will let you know once he gets here, I promise."

Cecil smiled and ran off to join the other children. Finally, finishing her cupcake, Kendra walked into the kitchen to throw away the cupcake wrapper when she heard a knock at the door. Mrs. Williams opened the door and Kendra saw a young boy with black hair and blue eyes with a woman carrying a pie. He looked like the boy that Cecil had described.

"I'm sorry," the woman said. "This must be the wrong house."

"No, it's not," the boy named James said, pointing to Kendra's brother as he continued to play with the other children. "Cecil is right there."

"Shush, James," the woman said, grabbing the boy's hand. She glared at her son. The boy fell silent. The woman looked at Mrs. Williams with a forced smile.

Mrs. Williams remained silent.

"I'm sorry," the woman said again. "He is mistaken. Have a nice day." The woman turned around and walked away with the boy. Every so

often, James would turn around to look at the house until he got into the car.

Mrs. Williams closed the door. Kendra stared at her mother who looked disappointed as she faced her smiling son who was still playing in the other room. Kendra threw away the cupcake wrapper and followed her mother into the living room. Her mother pulled Cecil to the side and whispered something that Kendra could not make out. A look of disappointment fell upon the boy's face and his smile quickly disappeared. Kendra felt sad as she watched her brother burst into tears. Mrs. Williams embraced her son. Kendra stepped forward to listen to their mother speak.

"It's okay, dear," she said. "Look at all your other friends who came. They came here to be with you and your sister. You can see your friend another time."

"But he promised that he would come," Cecil said.

"Sometimes things happen," Mrs. Williams said. "I'm sure he wanted to be here too, but he can't come to the party today. How about you and

I cut two pieces of cake for you and James to eat tomorrow at school? That way you two can still celebrate together. Would you like that?"

Cecil nodded, still somewhat disappointed, but walked with his mother and helped her to wrap the cake for both children to eat the following day.

"Hey," James whispered to Kendra in the art class, "can I have your number? I'm having a hard time with some of these projects, and I would appreciate the help."

"I don't give out my number," Kendra said, trying to stay focused on her assignment.

"Please," said James. "We are both in the art club. You're the vice-president. I thought you liked to help people, and Mrs. Montrell doesn't seem to like me. I really want to do better."

"But it doesn't even look like you're trying. We had plenty of time to do the work, but you were busy on your phone—like right now."

"I was trying to find out how to do the assignment, but I couldn't. I wouldn't be back in this class if I didn't want to try. I'm not as talented as you are, but if you helped me, I could be better...and then, maybe, Ms. Montrell will like me."

Kendra was irritated. She did not know if she should believe him or not. She had begun to notice that he would spend majority of the class time smiling and sneaking glances at her. It made her extremely uncomfortable. If she were to give him her number, she was unsure of what would happen next. However, he was correct about her duties as the vice-president of the art club which included helping members and he was a member. If he were to go back and tell Ms. Montrell or the president of the art club that she refused to help him, they might suggest that she should no longer be the vice-president. She had worked so hard to become the vice-president and thoughts of her losing her position would be a significant loss to her.

"Okay," Kendra said reluctantly as she keyed her number into his phone. "Long as I can help you with your work."

There was a knock at the door and James was called out. Finally, Kendra felt like she could breathe again. She wished that he had chosen to sit near another student. His presence had become too much of a distraction. She was behind on her project because she had to work her assignments for her other classes and they all were very demanding of her time, forcing her to fall behind and struggling to catch up with barely any extra time to spare.

James walked back into the classroom and sat down next to her again.

"You smell nice," he said. "Is it a peaches and vanilla scent?"

"Yes," said Kendra.

"It smells good on you. I like it."

Kendra stared nervously at her paper. She wondered why James kept on focusing on her and not his own work. She began to wonder if he was being sarcastic with his remarks, like many of the students had been in some of her other classes. It had been thirty minutes into the class, and he still had yet to complete anything on his paper other than his name. Ms. Montrell made her way between them.

"Looking good, Kendra," she said. "Your hard work is paying off. Make sure that you bring the strokes of your lines closer together to minimize any gaps between the colors."

"Yes, ma'am," said Kendra. She began to work on her project once again.

"James," Ms. Montrell said, now looking at his paper, "your paper is still blank. Is there anything you needed help with?"

"Kendra said she would help me," James said.

Kendra paused for a moment. He was completely relying on her help and was refusing help from the teacher. Kendra wanted to yell at him and remind him that he had told her that he wanted to do better in the class, yet his words and actions were once again proving that he was not making any efforts to seriously work on his project by himself.

"The teacher is right there," she thought. "Why can't you just let her help you? I am barely able to work on my project right now, much less yours."

"I can help you since I am right here," Ms. Montrell said.

"I don't want any help," James said.

"Well, I will come back around here later to check on you," Ms. Montrell said, walking away.

Kendra heard a groan from James.

"I am so sick of her," he whispered. "She is always getting on my case about everything. I don't see why she hates me so much. She is always complimenting everyone's work, but when it comes to me, she is nothing but negative."

Kendra remained silent, trying to ignore him and his endless complaining. She felt her phone vibrate in her pocket. She ignored it, not wanting to get in trouble with the teacher. She waited until the class ended before taking out her phone. She had received a text message from James.

James: Hey beautiful. 😊

Kendra stared at the phone and stuffed it back into her pocket. She was speechless. He had a crush on her! No wonder he had been acting strange, giving her compliments throughout the class, and insisted on sitting next to her at each possible moment he could get. Kendra wasn't sure about him. He had annoyed her and didn't seem to be the hardworking type of person that she would have liked within a relationship. Sure, he was handsome, but her parents have always instructed her since middle school to not focus on boys and to focus on school. He was already distracting and irritating her, and they weren't even seeing each other.

She made her way to her English honors class and sat down. The class was working on their individual research papers. As she opened her book to read, locks of blonde hair fell upon her book. Whitney Foster sat in front of Kendra and at any given moment, she liked to toss and push her hair towards the top of Kendra's desk.

"Excuse me," said Kendra. "Could you please stop doing that? Your hair is all over my desk and I need to read my book."

"And, so what?" said Whitney running her fingers through her hair and tossing it over her shoulder towards Kendra's area once again. Kendra scooted her desk back as far as she could and began to read her book. Soon, Whitney began to cough. Annoyed, several people in the class began to look at her. "What are you wearing? That perfume smells like bug spray. You need to take a bath and get rid of the smell."

"Whitney," the teacher, Mrs. Andrews, said. "Be considerate of your fellow classmates and be quiet so they can do their papers in peace."

"But her perfume is choking me," Whitney said. "How can I be quiet when I have to smell that?"

The teacher stared at Whitney until she finally decided to be quiet and work on her paper once again. Kendra looked down at her paper, hurt. She had been given that perfume by her mother to calm her down. She was suffering from extreme anxiety and had only told her parents a little bit about the stress that she was under. Yet, the demands of her classes were starting to get to the best of her, along with the bullying from her peers that she had not begun to tell anyone. She had only sprayed herself once with it daily to smell good and lift her spirits. Everyone had complimented the fragrance, except Whitney who usually had nothing nice to say about anything or anyone except her best friend, Beth Alvarez, who was also a member of the cheerleading squad. Kendra, like many of the 12th graders, did not like Whitney and usually avoided her at all costs. She was just unlucky to be one of the people to be sitting behind her because of the seating chart.

After class had ended, it was time to go to the gym and unfortunately it was at the same time as Whitney's gym class. As the girls began to change into their gym clothes, Whitney and Beth began to whisper amongst themselves, but loud enough for the other girls to hear.

"Her nose is so big, I can't see why she is having such a hard time smelling how strong her perfume is," Whitney laughed.

"I bet her hair isn't even real," Beth added.

Kendra ignored them, got into her gym clothes, and went to her class. She was happy that Whitney and Beth were in another class under another teacher but wished that the classes were at a different time. She hated having classes with them, like many other students, and had even witnessed Whitney getting into several fights with a girl named Jane Adams, who was the only one brave enough to actually fight Whitney.

"Ok, time for laps," the gym teacher, Mr. Holiday, said.

The class began their jog around the gym. Kendra ran with the rest of the class. She was trailing behind as the rest of the class took off ahead of her. She felt her confidence trailing. She was not a strong runner like her twin brother, Cecil. He always had been the more athletic one of the two. She ran as fast as she could but soon found herself quickly running out of breath. Her legs began to grow tired. She forced herself to run through the pain. Soon, she could not take it anymore and began to walk. She began to breathe heavily. The rest of the class was already finished, and she still had a few yards to go before reaching the area where the class was now gathered. She felt embarrassed. It felt like all eyes were on her, she was always last when it came to being athletic.

"C'mon, Kendra," Cecil shouted as his sister trailed behind him.

"I can't run any faster," Kendra shouted.

"I'm going to win," Cecil teased, now inches from the tree that they both agreed would be the finish line.

As Kendra got closer, Cecil finally tapped the tree and stuck his tongue out at her. He began to laugh as he always had done. He always liked to race and would always win, annoying his sister. No matter how many times they would play together, he could always run faster, jump higher, and do things that she was not as skilled in.

"I'm tired of racing," said Kendra. "Can't we just play something else?"

"What did you want to play?"

"Dolls," said Kendra.

"I don't want to play dolls. That's for girls."

"We can play catch."

"But that's for boys. Dad said so."

"But I want to play that!"

"Fine!" Cecil grabbed a ball and tossed it to his sister. It flew past her as she flinched. She ran after the ball and grabbed it. She tossed it back to her brother. It fell short inches between the two. Cecil ran forward, grabbed the ball, and tossed it again towards his sister. Still somewhat scared of the ball, Kendra froze, and the ball fell past her. Soon, Mr. Williams came out of the house, smiling. He grabbed the ball and began to toss it to his son, ignoring Kendra.

"I want to play too," said Kendra.

"Not now Kendra, I need to get Cecil ready for Little League," said Mr. Williams. "Go and play on the swing set. This is important."

Kendra frowned and did what she was told. It seemed like her brother was always looked upon *favorably by their dad. He was the apple of their father's eye, and he would spend extra time with Cecil making sure that he could run faster, jump higher, and much more. The only time Kendra would get anything close to that same look of approval from her dad was when she would bring home good grades. That was all that she could do. She was no athlete, nor did she feel special to him other than during those moments.*

Chapter 2

It was time to go to the cafeteria. Most of the students were separated, unfortunately, by race or cliques. Most of the white students sat with the white students, the black students sat with the black students, and so forth. There was one group, however, that was the only unique one called the Rainbows by the other groups. Kendra was part of the Rainbows. The Rainbow group had different people with various races in it who had been rejected by the other groups for various reasons. Most of the Rainbows got along with each other but were mainly loners outside of the group. Kendra had been rejected by the main black girl group of her school which was led by Jarika and Dominique. There were other blacks scattered in other groups according to cliques, including her own.

"*She is blackety black black,*" *Jarika Knowles said one day, eyeing Kendra.*

"*She also acts like she is white,*" *said Dominique. "She isn't one of us. I bet they only put her into those honors classes because she is a sellout. She probably thinks she is better than the rest of us."*

Those words hurt Kendra deeply. Sure, she was dark skinned, but that was something that she had no control over. She had always been taught to love her dark skin but was often hurt when her skin was the reason why so many of the other students bullied her. Additionally, she never felt that she was "acting white" and did not fully understand what the other students meant by that. To her, she had normal conversations and interactions with others as she would with her own family.

"Hey, Kendra," said Marie Kelly.

"Hi, Marie," Kendra said, sitting down next to her.

Marie was a mullato student who was going through something similar to what Kendra was going through by being rejected by both white and black groups, only she was fairer skinned. She was the president of the art club and was also talented in art. She and Kendra had known each other since the 9th grade, and both had worked hard to convince Ms. Montrell to start the art club so the art students could work on their own art projects and teach other students how to improve their skills. In fact, most of the kids from the Rainbow group were in the art club. There, most of the students felt that they could finally have a place where they were accepted.

"Ms. Montrell said that the new pottery wheels are finally in," Marie said. "She is going to show us how to use them so that we can help the other students later. She doesn't have a lot of them, so people might have to wait to take turns."

"Wow, this is going to be fun," said Kendra. She was excited. Ms. Montrell had placed an order for the pottery wheels, but they were on a back order since last school year. Now that they were in the possession of the school, they could finally learn how to do wheel throwing. Getting an early, firsthand demonstration by the teacher sounded like a big opportunity. She couldn't wait for the end of the school day to go back to the art room. She smiled from ear to ear.

Once school had ended, Kendra hurried to her locker and pulled out her apron. She put the apron on and looked at the inspirational stickers that were glued to the locker walls. The more she reviewed each sticker, the more encouraged she felt enough to bring a smile to her face. Now, it was time to bring that same energy to the art club. As soon as she closed the locker door, she saw James' face looking at her. Kendra jumped back in surprise to see him. He was smiling again as he leaned against the other lockers.

"You surprised me," Kendra said, trying to control her now racing heart.

"I'm here to walk you to the art room," James said.

"Um…okay," said Kendra as they both walked towards the art room. James walked ahead and opened the door for her. "Thanks." Once they both walked into the art room, some of the other art club members were working on their projects. Ms. Montrell and Marie were sitting in the back of the art room assembling the pottery wheels and were already in their aprons. Kendra placed her bag on one of the tables and walked to the back of the room to join them. James followed her.

Kendra stood by and listened as Ms. Montrell explained the different parts of the pottery wheel and how to operate it. James stood by yawning. He, then, sat down on a nearby chair. His eyes mainly were fixed on Kendra and once in a while, he would take a look at the demonstrations with little interest.

Ms. Montrell put a piece of clay in the center of the wheel and began to teach them how to center it. Kendra sat down and tried to center the clay, only to have the clay get off-center. Determined, she tried over and over again, eager to get it right. Finally, she got it centered. Wanting to practice again, she intentionally uncentered the clay and tried to center it once again.

"Just keep practicing and then we will move on," Ms. Montrell said, getting up to help other students in the art club.

Once the teacher was in the front of the classroom, James eyed Kendra and sat down next to her.

"That was boring," he said.

"Why are you always negative?" Kendra asked, trying to stay focused on her task. "At least she was nice enough to teach us how to center the clay. It's actually fun. Why don't you put on an apron and try to do it too? You might actually like it."

James grabbed an apron and put it in. He sat down again, grabbed some clay, and tried to center the clay. Soon, his clay spun off the wheel, getting remnants of clay on both him and Kendra. Frustrated, James took his foot off the pedal and looked at his apron.

"This sucks," he said. "I can't do this. It's all Ms. Montrell's fault."

"You have to keep practicing," Kendra said. "You only did it once. It's not going to go right on the first try."

"If she was a good teacher, it would have been," said James.

"I couldn't even do it on the first try."

"If you can't do it, how am I supposed to get it?"

"That's why we are all still practicing."

"James," Marie finally said, "If you don't like to wheel throw, you can always do something else."

"Like, what?" James fired back. "This club sucks. I thought I was going to be learning how to be better in art and all y'all have is have projects that I can't do, and I can't get any help."

"We are still learning how to do all of this ourselves," said Marie. "We've only been doing this for fifteen minutes. We can help you once we can get this. You can always go to Ms. Montrell and ask for help too."

"She doesn't like me."

"What makes you think that?" asked Marie. "Just go up and ask her. She is nice and helpful."

"I don't want to ask her," James said. "I'd rather have Kendra teach me."

"Kendra," Marie said. "Do you know enough to teach him yet?"

"I'm barely getting it myself," said Kendra. "We all are just going to have to wait for Ms. Montrell to finish helping other students to get more help."

James took off his apron and grabbed his bag.

"I'm leaving," he said. "Nobody wants me here and since I'm not wanted, I'm out."

Marie stared at the apron and the dirty pottery wheel that he left behind. She rolled her eyes and continued to practice centering the clay. A few minutes later, she looked at the clock and instructed the other students to clean up. Kendra hurriedly cleaned her wheel. She still needed to practice more and didn't feel comfortable teaching any other students something that she was having a hard time learning herself. Her eyes soon feel upon the dirty potter's wheel that James had left behind. She was upset because all of the art club members had been instructed to always clean up behind themselves and he had left his area a mess. Kendra began to clean up James' dirty area. Ms. Montrell walked to the back of the classroom. She said nothing and began to help Kendra clean up. They were past the time for the after-school activities. Kendra was mad at James. The art club members had never gone past the time before and would have been out on time if they did not have to clean up behind him.

"You can go ahead and go home," Ms. Montrell said. "I can finish cleaning up."

"It's okay," said Kendra, continuing to help.

Once they were finished, Kendra took off her apron and gathered her belongings. She walked down the hall, tired. There was no time to be tired, she had a research paper due tomorrow and had a test to study for. She quickly walked out of the building and began her walk home. She was glad that she lived only a block away from the school. She did not want to waste any more time.

She pulled out her key and unlocked the door to her home. As usual, her parents were still at their jobs, leaving her to fend for herself after school. She quickly fixed herself a sandwich and made her way to her room to work on her paper.

"I wish that I wasn't placed in all these honors classes," she thought. "I'm so stressed out. The students in the regular classes only need to site six sources, but my class has to site twelve and it's so much work. I only have ten and I need to find more sources. I wish that I could tell my parents that I don't want to be in these classes anymore and to just go back to the regular classes, but then, I would disappoint them, and the universities won't offer me as many opportunities... I wish I could just tell everyone that I am under so much stress. My only sanctuary is the art club, but now even that is getting stressful because of James."

After Kendra finished her paper, it was time to study for her test in the science class. It was now eight o'clock. She was tired and her eyes were getting heavy. She fought back the sleep until she couldn't any longer. Her eyes began to close, forcing her into a deep sleep.

"Look at my lil man," Mr. Williams said, "He is going to grow up and make us proud!"

Kendra watched as Mr. Williams continued teaching Cecil how to play baseball. He tossed the ball and was instructing Cecil how to hit it. Kendra was sitting next to her mother, with a book besides her. She walked up to her father, who was tossing another baseball to her brother, who was missing it.

"Can I play too?" she asked.

"Not now, Kendra," Mr. Williams said.

Kendra's head dropped low as she walked back to the porch next to her mother who was also reading a book. She grabbed the book that she was reading and began to read its contents. If she was not allowed to have fun in the real world, at least she could pretend to be someone else in a book who had endless possibilities in their world. She would read about their adventures, pretending to be the center of attention.

Kendra's eyes burst open. She looked at the clock on her desk. It was two o'clock in the morning and she had fallen asleep. She still had time to study. She quickly began to look at her notes from the science class. She began to feel overwhelmed as she got deeper and deeper into her studying. Soon, it was time for her to get ready to go to school. She quickly took a shower, put on her school uniform, and made her way into the kitchen where her parents were. Mrs. Williams had just finished placing the last plate on the table when Kendra sat down. It was a plate of grits, bacon, and eggs. Mr. Williams remained silent as he continued to eat.

"How is school going, Kendra?" asked Mrs. Williams.

"It's going pretty good," said Kendra. "I just finished working on my English paper and I have a science test today."

"I'm sure you will do great in both classes," said Mrs. Williams, smiling and sitting at the table to eat her plate of food. She had bags under her eyes from working at the grocery store and the gas station. She never complained about the shifts, but her physical features were telling. She always looked tired, forcing Kendra to think that if her parents are working so hard to make sure that she had what she needed in life, there would be no excuses for her to not work just as hard in school.

Mr. Williams on the other hand, used to smile a lot before working the construction job. He never really complained much before either. Lately, it seemed that he was having his own issues with the job that he had just taken as a means to earn extra income besides his other job at the store with Mrs. Williams.

"How are things going at the construction job, dear?" Mrs. Williams asked her husband.

"Things would be better if Boudreaux wasn't there with his gang of idiots," Mr. Williams said. "It is hard enough trying to find work in this town, but at every chance they can get, they are always trying to do things to make everyone's life miserable. I heard from one of the other workers that they don't like black people and the longest any of us ever lasted on that job in their department was a month. I am concerned about that, especially since people have complained about him before and he's still working there."

"Isn't his wife the principal at Kendra's school?" Mrs. Williams asked. "Kendra, how does Mrs. Boudreaux treat you at the school?"

"She hasn't given me a hard time, so far," said Kendra. "Sometimes she stands in the hallway with the teachers on duty, but I never had been called into her office for any trouble..."

"Didn't their son used to hang out with Cecil?" Mrs. Williams asked. "I'm trying to remember...I think I met her once at your birthday party...She had the son, but said she was at the wrong place or something. How does the son treat you?"

"He doesn't really do anything," said Kendra. "He hasn't said anything racial to me, but he likes to follow me around sometimes."

"Follow you?" Mr. Williams asked, raising an eyebrow.

"Yeah," said Kendra. "I think he might have a thing for me."

"Well, keep away from him," said Mr. Williams. "If he is anything like his father, he is rotten to the core. Be careful of the mother as well. They are not to be trusted."

Kendra wondered about what her parents were saying. Could it be true that the Boudreaux family were a racist family? She knew that James was following her around like a lovesick puppy, but he did not seem to be racist as her parents were saying and wondered how he could be racist when he was her brother's best friend many years ago. Sure, she could absolutely say that he was lazy and unmotivated in school, but if he had a crush on her and her being a different race than he was, how could he be racist?

Chapter 3

Kendra sat down in the hallway with the Rainbow group once again, eager for school to begin. She had finished her paper and still had a little more time to study for her science test. She took out her book and began to review the questions from the chapters. Things were starting to get confusing, and nothing was starting to make sense. She began to panic as the bell rang.

"I cannot fail this test!" she thought. "If I don't pass my grade will suffer. I wish that I would have gotten more sleep and would quit freaking out."

Her heart began to race as the clock began to tick, counting down the time to her next class. She felt her phone vibrate. She looked down to see that she had gotten a text message from James yet again.

James: Good morning, beautiful.

Kendra didn't know what to say or do. So far, he had been the one sending her text messages daily. She had not responded to any of his messages, yet he still was determined to speak to her. Her father had told her to keep away from him. When he wasn't complaining about things, he had seemed to be polite to her, but she wasn't sure how she felt about him. She never had the time to consider thinking about him much. Her main focus had been school, but right now, she needed a distraction.

Kendra: Hey

James: Oh, so now you answer. Lol, I'm glad. Would you like to go out on a date?

Kendra: I can't. I'm not allowed to date.

James: You are in the 12th grade. Certainly, your parents aren't that strict, are they?

Kendra: They are. I know you like me and all, but I cannot date you. I'm sorry.

James: Why not?

Kendra: I'm not allowed to date and I'm too busy to date anyone right now.

James: Tell me the truth, it's because I'm white, huh?

Kendra: No, I'm telling the truth. I don't have time for a relationship and can't be in one.

James: You could make time if you really wanted to. Just give me a chance. I really want to be with you more than anything.

Kendra: I can't. I'm sorry.

The bell rang and the students began to walk out of the classroom. Kendra placed her phone back into her pocket and made her way to her next class. Her eyes fell upon James out in the hallway, but she did not have time to talk to him and continued her dash to class. She had a test. While going through the hallway. She heard some of the kids making fun of Ms. Montrell by calling her, "Ms. Monty," including James. She felt angry because Ms. Montrell was her favorite teacher, but she still had to go to her class, and she reluctantly did so.

"Good luck everyone," the science teacher said, handing out the last test. "Just remember what we've reviewed and I'm sure you all will do well."

Kendra looked at her test. As the teacher said, it was based upon what was reviewed earlier in class, yet it did have some formulas that took her some extra time to solve. Once she finished her test, she flipped her test over and waited for the rest of the class to finish. The other students kept working quietly. It started to get boring, so Kendra turned her test back over and began to review her answers. She kept getting the same answers and hadn't missed any questions. She flipped the test back over. Minutes later, the teacher instructed the class that the time was over and collected the papers.

There was a sharp kick to the back of Kendra's desk. Kendra turned around to see Whitney glaring at her.

"I hope you fail," she said.

"Same to you," Kendra said, scooting her chair forward away from Whitney. Whitney stopped and stared Kendra down once the bell rang for the class to end. She slightly pushed the desk with her hip and walked out of the classroom. Kendra moved her desk back and followed the rest of the students out into the hallway where most of the football players at the school had begun to call Ms. Montrell the nickname throughout the school. Kendra began to wonder why they would do such a disrespectful act. She felt that Ms. Montrell was a good teacher and did not deserve to be mistreated the way that she was being mistreated. It did not seem to be fair, and she was disappointed to see that James was one of the people participating in the heckling. She wanted to talk to James and ask him why he was choosing to partake in the act after the teacher had tried her best to work with him.

"Why are you so mean to Ms. Montrell?" she asked him.

"Because it's fun," he said. "She makes the class harder than it has to be because she wants us to be like you, and it's not fair."

"You don't even turn in any work. Why are you comparing yourself to me anyway? I worked hard for my grade. I offered to help you several times, and you still don't do any work. I thought you said you wanted to do better this year, and all you've managed to do was turn the whole school against Ms. Montrell. That's not right."

"It's not right for her to not like us."

"Maybe she would like you if you and the others didn't call her 'Ms. Monty' or treat her like crap."

James stared at Kendra. Kendra couldn't help but look disappointed. He looked disappointed as well. She turned away and walked to her next class. She began to think that maybe he was the cruel person as her father had warned her about. If that were the case, she wanted to have nothing to do with him. There were people that she didn't like as well, but she never thought that it would right for a person to mistreat others, especially if it was undeserved.

After school, it was time for art club to begin. She grew angry at seeing James. She still couldn't believe that he took enjoyment out of being cruel to others and she could barely even look at him. Her witnessing the heckling done by him and his friends made her feel disgusted to her core. She turned away, hoping that he would take it as a hint that she was not interested in talking to him.

"Hey, you," he said.

Kendra couldn't help but frown at the sight of him. She avoided looking at him further as she opened her locker to gather her things.

"I know we already talked about his earlier," James said. "But I was wondering, if you'd like to go out sometime?"

"No, thanks," Kendra said closing her locker.

"Why not?" James leaned against her locker, looking at her. "I think we have a lot in common. We're both in the art club. You like me; I like you."

"Yes, we're both in the art club, but that's it. We don't have anything in common. You like me, but I don't like you. You're mean to others. You are lazy in and out of class. You don't hold yourself accountable for your actions, and you bully other people and get others to bully for you."

Kendra then looked at James whose face was now red in anger. She was angry too. Seeing that there was nothing more to discuss, she turned away and walked into the art room, hoping that he would now leave her alone. He didn't follow her into the art room that day and she was glad that he didn't.

"What happened to your boyfriend?" Marie asked Kendra as she put on an apron and sat down next to her.

"He's not my boyfriend," Kendra corrected her, trying to center her clay. She hated seeing other students being disrespectful to her favorite teacher. She looked up to see Ms. Montrell sitting at her desk, looking somewhat withdrawn. She didn't go around helping the students during the art club as she would usually do. Instead, she was at her desk grading projects with a look of hurt in her eyes. Kendra felt sorry for Ms. Montrell and grew angrier at James and his friends. Once it was time for the art club to end, she waited for the last student to exit the classroom before walking up to Ms. Montrell's desk.

"Ms. Montrell," she said. "Thank you for all that you do to help us and I'm glad that you are my favorite teacher."

"Thanks, Kendra," said Ms. Montrell.

Kendra for a moment, saw a flash of hope in her teacher's sad eyes. She wished that there was more that she could do. She decided to make a card for the teacher and have the art club students sign it to show their appreciation for her and everything she had taught them. She smiled as she walked out the door to hurry home and work on the card.

Chapter 4

"Good job, Kendra," Mrs. Andrews said, giving Kendra back her research paper the following day. Kendra had gotten an A+ on it. Kendra smiled and reached into her bag to grab her folder. She still had two more tests that week and once she would be finished with them, she could finally take a break from studying and be a little less stressed about her grades.

"I bet you plagiarized the whole thing," Whitney said, looking at her. "You're not fooling me. The only reason why she gave you a good grade was because you're black and blacks can't make good grades like that."

"Shut up and leave me alone," Kendra told her, annoyed.

"I bet my paper was better than yours," Whitney continued. "It's not fair that I got a B and you got a higher grade than me. I want to see your paper!"

"You only got a B because your paper was not as good as mine," Kendra fired back. "Turn around and shut up. I'm tired of you!"

Other students had begun to look their way, surprised that Kendra was finally standing up to Whitney. Mrs. Andrews made her way to the girls and made Whitney switch her seating with another student, putting her further away from Kendra. Kendra couldn't have been happier to see Whitney be moved to another seat.

Unfortunately, for Kendra, she did not do as well on her science test. She had made a B grade on the test, dropping her grade by a few points into a low A in the class. Kendra felt her heart go into a panic. She didn't want to disappoint her family. She had struggled to keep her straight A's in all her classes and now she was going to have a B if she didn't work harder. She felt added stress and her head began to hurt. During lunch, she felt the need to talk to Marie. She was the only person she felt that she could trust enough to talk to about her pressures.

"I don't think one B is going to hurt," Marie said. "Honors classes are hard to make A's in anyway. You are gifted if you are able to make those types of grades in those classes. I was lucky to get into one honors class. I wish that we were in the same class though. That would have been sweet."

"Yeah, but people don't even like me in those classes," said Kendra. "People think that I cheat and give me a hard time because I'm black. They don't think that I earned any of my grades and don't think of all the hard work I've done to get to where I am."

"I get a hard time too," said Marie. "I am too black for whites and too white for blacks. It's a lose-lose situation to not be accepted by either group. At least we have our club to go to after school where people don't care about skin color."

"Yeah, but people are even starting to give Ms. Montrell a hard time," Kendra added. "They are being mean to teachers just like the students. I wish that things weren't the way that they are. I wish that more could be done about it to make good changes."

During the art class, Kendra was upset to see that James was still sitting in his usual spot next to her. She didn't want to sit next to him and be bothered with his lazy ways. She noticed that one of the students who sat in the back of the classroom was absent that day and decided to sit there instead. She noticed that James eyed her with curiosity as he watched her go to the back of the classroom. Soon, there was a flash of rage in his eyes. He glared at the boy that was sitting next to her. He eagerly raised his hand when Ms. Montrell asked for volunteers to pass back the projects. When he was chosen to pass back the papers, he angrily looked at Kendra once he returned her paper and slammed down the project to the guy who was sitting next to her, looking even more furious.

"What's your problem?" the boy asked him.

James said nothing and continued to angrily look at the boy, staring him down. He shoved the table slightly as he continued to pass back the papers. Once he finished, he threw himself into his chair in the front of the classroom, refusing to talk to anyone and refusing to do any work. Every so often, he would look to the back of the classroom. Finally, he pulled something out of his pocket and began to look downwards. Kendra felt her phone vibrate. She received several text messages from James.

James: Oh, so that is the real reason why you didn't want to date me.

James: You can date him, but not me?! What's so good about him? He's nothing special.

James: I knew you were lying! All that talk about having strict parents and being busy were lies!

James: It was only a matter of time before I knew the truth.

James: Are you sleeping with him too?

James: I bet you are!

James: Well, the joke is on you; I have two girlfriends. You would have only been the third.

James: You girls are all same. You are only good for one thing!

Kendra's eyes grew wide with anger as she shoved her phone into her pocket. She was really upset with James. He had two other girlfriends and was trying to get her to date him as well. Her head began to spin. She wasn't even dating anyone, and he was upset at her and even confessed his true intentions. She watched as he stormed out the classroom after class ended. In the hallways, people looked in curiosity as James began to punch a few lockers as he made his way down the hall. Frustrated, Kendra groaned and went to her next class.

For the next few days, James refused to speak to her, even when she was forced to sit next to him again during the art class. He didn't show up to the art club sessions either. Kendra felt no guilt or remorse. She had done nothing to him and felt no need to go out of her way to make him feel better about himself. He would still shoot glances at the other boy in the back of the classroom, thinking that there was something going on between him and Kendra. He was still angry that Kendra had sat next to him in the classroom. He had even gone as far as calling Ms. Montrell his nickname for her in front of the class, which always landed him a detention which he felt no remorse in receiving.

"I want to know the truth," he said, one day after class. "Are you still seeing him?"

"I already told you, I'm not seeing anyone," Kendra said, walking down the hall.

"Why can't it be me?" he demanded. "I've asked you many times and you are always acting like you don't want to be bothered."

"Don't you have two other girlfriends to be worrying about?" Kendra reminded him.

"I don't want either of them," James said. "I only want you. I will get rid of them if you get rid of your boyfriend and date me instead."

"For the last time, I am not dating anyone," Kendra said. "I only sat down in another seat next to another boy once and you made a big deal out of nothing. When have you ever seen me be affectionate with anyone? Never! I'm not holding hands with anyone. I'm not kissing anyone. Nothing! You need to just stop acting possessive. Earlier in the school year, you said that you wanted to do better, but you never do. You don't work hard in school, and you are mean to other people, especially Ms. Montrell and it's sickening. You have a very low opinion of women saying that they are only good for one thing. Then, lets add to the fact that you are dating two other girls and trying to get me to date you as well. If I dated someone like you, especially knowing what I know now about you, what would that make me? You make me sick with how you act. I just wish that you would just go away."

Kendra quickened her pace, leaving him behind. She said nothing further to him, even after school during the art club when he showed up. He didn't sit as close to her as before, but sat in the front of the classroom, looking at her with some hurt in his eyes. He remained silent, sitting as if he were a child in a timeout. Finally, he rose from the spot where he had been sitting and walked out of the classroom.

Chapter 5

Running down the hallway, Kendra finally stopped in front of her locker. She had just finished taking another test and was running behind again. She quickly put her books in her locker and gathered her art supplies. Once she closed her locker, she found James leaning against the lockers, looking at her. She waited for him to have another one of his tantrums, but he remained silent as if waiting for her to give him some verbal cue.

"Yes, James?" she said forcing a smile.

"I don't like how things ended the last time we talked. I thought about what you said, and I will do better to be a better person. I even did my homework last night. I won't even give Ms. Montrell a hard time anymore."

"Yeah, for how long?"

"I see that you're still upset," he sighed. "I will prove myself. I will be as quiet as a mouse and do my work...All those other things I said...I didn't mean them. I would never use you. I even broke up with the other girls because I only want you. If you make me your boyfriend, I will dedicate my all just for you. I love you and only you."

Kendra began to feel extremely uncomfortable around him. She felt that she had to get away from him. James grabbed her hand and kissed it. He laced his fingers between hers and walked her to the classroom. Once there, Kendra let go of his hand and made her way to Ms. Montrell's desk.

"Ms. Montrell," she said. "Could I please be excused to see Mrs. Boudreaux?"

"Sure, Kendra," said Ms. Montrell.

Kendra turned around to see James sitting quietly in the desk next to hers. She forced a smile as she left the room. Her heart began to race at the thought of being possessed by James. She walked into the office and asked to speak to Mrs. Boudreaux. Mrs. Boudreaux was in her office with another student, so she had to wait before being called into the office. Once it was her turn, she sat down nervously on the other side of Mrs. Boudreaux's desk. She knew that she had to choose her words very carefully. Her parents had warned her about the family being prejudiced and she didn't want to make things worse.

"How may I help you, Kendra?" Mrs. Boudreaux asked.

"I know it's a little late in the semester," Kendra said, "But, could I please be put into another art class?"

"May I ask why?"

"To be honest, I just don't feel comfortable in the third period class. I would feel more comfortable in the fifth-period class."

"What is making you uncomfortable? Is it Ms. Montrell or another student?"

"It's not Ms. Montrell. I actually like her class. I am uncomfortable with being in the same class as another student. I don't really want to say who it is. I just want to be able to work in peace."

"I'll see what I can do. If you switch classes, it will have to begin starting tomorrow. I think it should be okay."

"Thank you."

Kendra waited for Mrs. Boudreaux to key in her new schedule. Once she was handed the new schedule, she walked back to class to see James anxiously waiting for her. He smiled as she sat down.

"See," he said, showing her his work. "I told you that I was going to work on my assignment."

"Good for you," she said.

"Do me a favor," James said. "Think about what I said and let me know what you decide. I meant what I said when I told you that I loved you. I will do anything to make you happy. Just tell me what you want, I don't care what it is, I will do it for you."

Kendra felt terrified. She knew that she had already changed her schedule, but he did not know that. She had already seen an example of his wrath when he was jealous of her sitting by another male student. She didn't even want to think about how he would react once he found out about her schedule change. She began to shiver.

"Do you want my jacket?" James asked, noticing her shaking.

"I'll be okay," Kendra said.

"Here," James placed his jacket over her, unaware that she was only shivering in fear and not by the temperature. Every once in a while, he would wrap his arm around her as they sat down and pushed his chair closer to hers all the while smiling. Once the bell had rung, he grabbed their papers and turned it in. Kendra handed him back his jacket. "You can keep it if you want."

"No, thanks," said Kendra, grabbing her bags and handing him the jacket.

James quickly grabbed his bag and ran after her. He quickly grabbed her hand. Kendra felt defeated. He, now more than ever, was getting more and more possessive and clingy. She wanted to just go to class in peace. She didn't want to have a boyfriend, much less someone who was trying to force themselves into her life. Before she could walk into her next class, James held firmly to her hand and pulled her towards him. He embraced her and held her.

"I love you," he whispered into her ear, before letting her go. Kendra wanted to scream but kept her thoughts to herself as she walked into her next class. She felt like a trapped insect caught in a spider web. Any movement she would make, it seemed like he was there. She felt like she couldn't breathe without worrying. Once the bell rang, she was glad that he was gone, and she was able to be in her next class without him.

"What are you doing with James?" Whitney demanded, looking at her from her desk.

"None of your business," Kendra said, walking to her desk on the other side of the classroom.

"I'm making it my business," Whitney said from across the room.

"Whitney, class has begun," the teacher said, silencing her.

"I guess she must be one of his girlfriends," Kendra thought. "I don't feel like getting into anymore drama with her or him. How did I even end up in this situation anyway? No wonder my parents told me to not get involved with anybody in high school. At this rate, I don't see myself ever dating anyone period."

During class, even though Whitney sat across from her, she still would try to do what she could to make Kendra's life miserable in the class. Whenever Kendra answered a question given by the teacher, Whitney would pretend to cough.

"S-Slut," she coughed each time Kendra would answer a question.

"Shut up," Marie finally said, irritated.

"Make me, bitch," Whitney said.

"Whitney," the teacher said, "You are being very disrespectful. You are getting a detention."

"I don't care," Whitney said. "She is a slut and I'm going to let everyone know."

"What did she do to you?" Marie demanded.

"She is trying to steal my boyfriend," Whitney said.

Some of the students in the class gasped while others began to snicker. All eyes suddenly fell upon Kendra who was now embarrassed by the accusation. The students began to whisper and talk amongst themselves while the teacher, unsuccessfully, tried to get the class to refocus on the class lesson for the day.

"Wwwwwoooowwww," Jarika said. "I knew it. She really does want to be white, huh."

"Girl, it's always the dark-skinned ones or the light brights," added Dominique. "They never want to be black. At any chance, they try to whiteout anything black."

"That's not true," Kendra snapped back. "I'm not trying to steal anyone's boyfriend and I'm not trying to be white! I just want everyone to leave me alone!"

"Everyone, get back to work," the teacher ordered.

"Well, she will never be white," Whitney continued. "No matter how many white guys she dates."

"Whitney," the teacher said. "Do you want to be suspended? You already got a detention. If you don't stop disturbing my class, you will be asked to leave."

Kendra finally burst into tears. She was humiliated in front of the whole class. Now everyone was sneaking glances at her and whispering. She was glad that she was having her schedule changed. She prayed that none of the other students would be in most of her other classes. She had been labeled as a boyfriend stealing slut, someone who hated being black, and much more, all none of her doing. She was rejected by all, once again. Even Marie was looking down at her desk with anger and embarrassment. Kendra felt bad for her as well. They had no place outside of the Rainbow group.

After school, Kendra was still depressed. She did not show up for the art club. She couldn't even face her friends as she began to notice other students whispering about her once she crossed their paths. She just wanted to go home and not go back to school. She felt her heart break as she began to hate herself and her dark skin.

Kendra wiped the tears away from her face as she approached her family's house. Surprisingly, her father's vehicle was parked in the driveway. She wondered why he was back so soon. His shift usually didn't end until much later. She took out her key, unlocked the door, and walked in.

"Dad?" she said, seeing him on the couch.

"Kendra," Mr. Williams said, with sorrow in his voice.

"What are you doing home early?" she asked.

"I lost my job," her father said. "They were having cutbacks at the store. Your mother's job was even eliminated. She is out at her other job at the gas station. Things are going to be very tight until we both can find stable employment again. I didn't want to tell you, but it looks like we might have to move if we cannot find more employment here. I still have work at the construction company, but it was only part time."

"I'm sorry, dad," Kendra said, hugging her father. She could see the hurt in his eyes. He had worked hard only to be let go of the company that he had been working at for years. "I can look for an after-school job."

"Absolutely not," said Mr. Williams. "Your school comes first for you. Let your mother and I worry about finding work. We will come up with something. How did your day go?

Kendra remained silent. She wanted to be honest with her father about the hard time that she was having at school. She wanted to tell him how she was being bullied and harassed. She also wanted to say that her classes were overwhelming her, but at least she managed to change her schedule.

"Things are fine," she lied, feeling guilty soon afterwards.

"I'm glad," her father said. "You make your mother and me proud. You are a hard worker and don't worry, your mother and I will see to it that you make it into a good college one way or the other, just make sure that you keep your grades up."

"I will," Kendra said, forcing a smile.

Chapter 6

The next day, Kendra started her new schedule. She was still in the same homeroom class, but her classes were switched with some of the same teachers. She was happy to still be in her art class at a different time. She would have hated to have that class dropped most of all. She prayed that she would not have many classes with Whitney, Jarika, or Dominique. People began to whisper as she walked down the hall. As usual, she ignored them and went straight to her locker and gathered her books for her first few classes. She sat down with her usual group of friends. Well, at least most of them. Some of the members were missing, but Kendra did not think much of it. Sometimes, some of the people would sit by themselves for a period time and return later. Kendra noticed that Marie still had a sad look upon her face. She knew that Marie hated the racism that was prevalent in the school. She hated it herself and that was one of the reasons why both girls had bonded in the 9th grade.

"Hi," Kendra said.

Marie said nothing. She refused to talk to anyone and just stared at the floor. The rest of the kids in their group also sat down in silence. Soon, Kendra felt something smack her on the cheek. It was a scrunched-up piece of paper.

"Boyfriend stealer," someone shouted from the crowd.

Kendra stared at the paper, not knowing who had thrown it. Kids were walking up and down the hallway. Someone proceeded to kick her in the legs as they walked by. Kendra tucked in her legs further, trying to hold back the tears.

"Imitation white," another voice called out from the crowd.

Most of the kids from the Rainbow group began to look uncomfortable as other groups of students began to gather. More of the rainbow kids slowly began to sit in other random parts of the hallway until it was only Marie and Kendra sitting by themselves in the usual spot on the floor.

The bell rang.

Marie remained silent as she made her way to her next class. She didn't bother to even talk to Kendra before she left, like she would normally do. Kendra felt alone. She went to her homeroom and sat down. The other students continued to whisper around her.

"You thought those white folks were gonna accept you, huh?" Dominique asked her. "Looks like you got to learn the hard way."

"You know what," Jarika added. "It all makes sense now. Since she is dating the principal's son, that's how she was able to get all those A's in those honors classes. I bet she is really as dumb as rocks."

"Just leave me alone," Kendra said. "None of that is even true. I'm not even dating anyone, and my grades are from my hard work, nothing else."

"That's a lie," someone shouted from across the room. "I saw her holding hands with James out in the hall yesterday."

"He was even all hugged up on her like this," a boy said, holding himself. Some of the students began to laugh.

"Yeah, her hard work was getting' him to like her," Dominique laughed. "I don't see why she wants him. He barely has any lips to kiss." More and more eyes fell upon Kendra as more students began to laugh. Some students were even crying from laughing so much. Kendra began to shake. She began to reach for her hair but forced her hands back down to her sides. Kendra was embarrassed. Yes, she and James had held hands in the hallway, but he had held her hand that day. He was trying to force her into a relationship with him. She never told him nor anyone else that they were dating or that she was interested in seeing him in that way. It wouldn't matter what she thought anyway because most of the class perceived her as being in a relationship with him and there was nothing that she could do to sway their opinions. Kendra's phone began to vibrate.

"I bet that's her white boyfriend," Jarika said, looking down at Kendra's pocket.

"Don't you have better things to do than to mess with me?" Kendra asked.

"Take your phone out," another student said. "We wanna see if it's him or not."

"She ain't gonna do it," someone else said. "She gonna be more exposed then!"

Upset, Kendra walked to the front of the classroom and sat down in an empty seat. She wished that her homeroom class was switched out. Nobody liked her in her homeroom class, and everyone was thinking that she was involved in things that were not true. She prayed that the rest of her day would not go as bad as her homeroom was going. Once the bell rang for the students to go to their next class, she looked at her phone. It was another text message from James.

James: Good morning, beautiful

Kendra jammed the phone into her pocket. She did not want to deal with anyone right now and was extremely irritated. She stomped her way to her next class, wishing that the day would hurry up and end. As the day continued, she was relieved to learn that she had no more classes with Whitney. However, regrettably, she had gym with both Dominique and Jarika. She switched out one problem for another. She felt that she could not win.

During her fifth period art class, she sat down in the last empty seat next to a boy. She began to panic because the person was white, and she had been bullied all day by her peers about being around white boys. However, there were no other free seats. She reluctantly sat down next to him. She waited for him to tease her like the other kids had in her other classes, but the boy didn't. He seemed to be more focused on working on his project more than anything else. After waiting a few minutes of silence, Kendra felt a little more at ease, nobody in the class as teasing her. She felt like she could finally breathe. There was no James or other students from her other classes in this one to make fun of her.

Once school had ended, Kendra made her way to the art club and was disappointed to see that James was there waiting for her. He was running his fingers through his hair and tapping his foot impatiently. If other students would see her with him again, she knew that the bullying would only get worse. Soon, his eyes locked onto hers and his anxious behavior subsided.

"I didn't see you in class third-period," he said.

"I'm sorry, but I'm no longer in that class."

"Why not?"

"I'd rather not say," Kendra grabbed her sculpture that she had been working on. "I have to work on my sculpture."

James rose from his usual spot and sat down next to her. He began to text on his phone for a few minutes before taking out his project to work on it. Kendra wished that he would sit somewhere else. His presence around hers was one of the causes of her being bullied and she felt embarrassed to have him near her again. Whenever she would move to another area to get tools, he would look up from his paper and watch what she was doing. His eyes would only go back towards his paper once she would sit down near him. Kendra heard some snickering at the door. She looked up to see both Jarika and Dominique pointing at her through the glass window. She lowered her head, defeated.

Later that night, once she got to bed, she thought about the events. She wanted the teasing and harassment to stop. Even though she knew that James liked her, she had to get away from him. It would be the only way to cool things down and stop the rumors from spreading. She looked down at her pocket as her phone began to vibrate once again. It was more text messages from James.

James: Hey…

James: Talk to me.

James: Did you leave the third-period class because of me? What did I do?

James: I'm sorry if you dislike me.

James: You don't like me because I'm a white guy who likes black chicks?

James: I am not that bad once you get to know me. I will never hurt you.

James: Look, I really like you. You are beautiful, smart, and smell nice. I'd really like to go out with you if you'd just give me a chance. I can't stop thinking about you.

James: I won't stop texting you until you talk to me.

James: Stop ignoring me!

Kendra stared at her phone and burst into tears. She just wanted to be left alone. She didn't want to be caught up in anymore drama from James, Jarika, Whitney, Dominque, and other people from the school. She only wanted to go to school and make her family proud. She needed to talk to someone, but she couldn't go to her parents. They were already under a lot of pressure trying to find jobs to help support the family. Kendra felt like she was out of options.

"I can't take this anymore," Kendra thought to herself, crying. "I need help. I want things to go back to the way they were before all of this drama even happened. I can't go to my parents or my friends. The only person that I can think of is Mrs. Gonzalez. I hope that she will be able to help me. I can't deal with this on my own."

Chapter 7

"Good morning, Kendra," Mrs. Gonzalez said as Kendra sat down in a chair across from the counselor. "What brings you in today?"

Kendra burst into tears. Surprised, Mrs. Gonzalez handed her some tissue. Kendra began to gasp as she choked between the sobs.

"Calm down," Mrs. Gonzalez said. "Take a deep breath."

Kendra felt her heart racing and her chest began to rapidly go up and down. She closed her eyes as she tried to calm herself down. The tears that she had been holding in for a long time were finally falling out of her eyes in rapid succession. She pressed the tissue against her eye lids and reached for another piece of tissue.

"I'm tired," she sobbed. "I'm tired of being bullied...I can't take it anymore."

"Who is bullying you?" Mrs. Gonzalez asked.

"Whitney, Jarika, and Dominque," Kendra said. "They have been making my life miserable. I try to be a good student and peer. I go to class and do my work and at any chance, they try to spread rumors about me that are not true. Now some of the other kids are targeting me and throwing papers at me."

"What kind of rumors are they spreading?"

"They are saying that I am in a relationship with James Boudreaux," Kendra said. "I'm not dating him, but he likes me and follows me around. Sometimes, I just wish he would stop doing that so that the other students will leave me alone. When people see me with him, Whitney, Jarika, and Dominique tell other people that I am trying to be white when I am not. Then, they are saying that because they think that I am dating him that that's the only reason why my grades are the way that they are and are calling me a boyfriend stealer. I just want all of these rumors and bullying to stop, especially with Whitney, Jarika, and Dominique. When it comes to James, I don't want to hurt his feelings or anything, but I need for him to understand that I'm not trying to date anyone right now. When I tried to talk to him before, he got angry with me. He is already upset with me and sent me text messages last night. I'm scared to talk to him because I don't need more enemies at the school."

"Would it be possible for me to read the text messages that he sent you?"

Kendra took out her phone and showed it to the counselor. Ms. Gonzalez looked back at Kendra and at the phone.

"Kendra," she said, give me a moment and I will be right back. She walked out of her office and walked into Mrs. Boudreaux's office for a few minutes and spoke with her. Then she walked back into the office with Kendra and closed the door.

"I will talk to all the of the students that are involved," she said. "You are brave to open yourself up to me about the bullying issue and I will do my best to help resolve the issues with the other students."

"Thank you," said Kendra, rising up from her seat.

Mrs. Gonzales called James, Whitney, Dominque, and Jarika over the intercom to go to the office. As she was doing so, Kendra began to delete the text messages sent by James. Once she looked up from her phone, she saw that James entered the office. He looked at her and sat down as she ran out.

Chapter 8

During the art class, Kendra had finally gotten her emotions under control. She had been crying throughout most of the day and had avoided looking at James, Whitney, Jarika, and Dominque throughout the day. She was now in her quiet art class with Ms. Montrell. The class was working on their projects quietly. Kendra heard a phone vibrating. It wasn't her phone. It was sound of the phone vibrating from the boy that was sitting next to her, Eric Keller. He took out his phone and began to read his text messages. Kendra looked back down at her paper and continued to work on her assignment. Suddenly a scrunched piece of paper flew between him and Kendra, missing them. Then there was a loud random screeching sound coming from the back of the classroom. Students from the middle and back of the class turned around and looked in the direction of a student named Derrick Johnson. He looked around behind himself and looked confused.

"Who threw this paper and made that noise?" Ms. Montrell demanded, picking up the paper.

The class remained silent.

"Whoever did that needs to stop," Ms. Montrell said. "This is a classroom, not your home. Be respectful!"

The class was quiet. Soon, students began to refocus on their assignments. Then, there was the sound of someone coughing from the back of the classroom and then some coughing from the front of the classroom.

"Ms. Monty," coughed a voice from the front of the classroom.

The class ignored it until it happened again.

"Ms. Monty," coughed the voice again.

Ms. Montrell rose from her chair behind her desk and glared at the class.

"Stop this behavior at once," she said.

Kendra's eyes began to fill with tears once again. She had prayed that she had left that negativity behind. Now, it was beginning to seem as though things were getting worse. First, she had to deal with James making fun of her favorite teacher, now she was in a class with more students who were beginning to misbehave. She still had some left-over tissue from the time that she had spent in Mrs. Gonzalez's office. She began to wipe the tears away with the tissue as the voices continued to heckle both the teacher and her.

"Wannabe white," someone called out.

"Black booger," someone coughed.

"Enough of this!" Ms. Montrell said, looking at the class, scanning the room to see who is making the verbal assaults.

The bell rang.

More distressed than ever, Kendra quickly walked out of the classroom. She still had two more classes to go to. She couldn't find the strength to go to class. She slumped down in the hallway as more students walked past her. She sat on the ground, frozen. The bell rang. She was alone in the hallway, for the first time, missing her class. She pulled her legs up to her chin and began to cry.

Chapter 9

"How was school today?" Mr. Williams asked Kendra as she walked through the door.

For the first time, Kendra didn't want to answer her father's question. She wanted to walk past him and go to her room. She hated school and what it had become to her. She hated people and didn't want to talk to anybody, including her parents. She had talked to others before, and things only got worse. Yet, since everything was out of control beyond her reach, she felt that she no longer had anything to lose. It no longer mattered to her if her parents knew or not. She was tired of everything at this point. She took a deep breath as her father looked up from the paper at her.

"It's horrible," Kendra said finally, revealing her truth. "I hate school. All people do is make fun of me. They call me names, accuse me of stealing boyfriends, and tell me that I'm trying to be white. I tried to change my schedule and all its done was make things worse. I hate everyone!"

"When did all of this start to happen?" Mr. Williams demanded, looking angry for the first time in a long time.

"It's been going on a while," said Kendra, crying. "I just go to school, try do my work, and everyone just finds a way to bully me for no reason."

"Is it the white kids that are doing this?" asked Mr. Williams.

"It's both the white and black kids."

"Is that James Boudreaux behind all of this?"

"Indirectly he is," said Kendra. "He has been following me around and then when the other students see that they tell me that I am trying to be white because they see him around me. But they had been doing that before he got into the picture, but now that he is around, it's gotten worse. It's not just him. There is this girl named Whitney who kept on accusing me of dating him and said that I stole him from her. Then there are these two girls named Jarika and Dominque who are accusing me of wanting to be white and say that my grades aren't real because they think that I am dating James."

"I'm gonna go and talk to the principal of that school tomorrow," Mr. Williams said. "I'm not going to sit around and let all of this happen. I don't care what race people are and if Mrs. Boudreaux gives me a hard time or blows this off, I'm going to head to the school board."

"But what if things get worse?" asked Kendra. "I tried to fix things and it got even more out of control. Nothing seems to be working."

"Things are only going to get worse for them," Mr. Williams said. "They should be the ones worried, not you. Since I have a lot of time on my hands right now, they are going to be hearing from me."

Kendra waited in the living room as her father called the school to set up an appointment to have a conference with the principal. Soon, he came back into the room and sat down next to his daughter with a concerned look on his face.

"I am going to do my best to get this taken care of," he said. "I don't want you to go back to that school, to be honest. Leave it to me. This is going to be resolved one way or the other. Just give me some time to work on it."

Chapter 10

Kendra looked at the floor that used to be occupied by the students in the rainbow group. Nobody was there in the morning and haven't been for the last few days. Slowly the others began to find ways to either find a spot to sit by themselves or talk their way into another group that shared similar activities after begging their way in. Kendra was now alone. Even the members of the art club were beginning to become fewer. At one point in time, they had almost a classroom size number of students, now it was down to their last five members and getting fewer. It was only a matter of time until the art club would no longer have its members, disappointing Kendra. Both she and Marie had done so much work trying to recruit the students throughout the years, only to be abandoned by them.

"This is all your fault," Marie told Kendra one day after school, while they were alone in the hallway. "If you didn't date James none of this would have happened. Now the club is practically gone. I don't even want to be president anymore."

"But none of what people are saying is true," said Kendra. "I didn't do anything. I didn't date anyone, steal anyone's boyfriend, or try to be something that I am not. I'd expect that from the others, but not from you."

"If it's not true, then why are so many people saying that you are lying about the situation?" asked Marie. "Did you know that people are going around saying that you hate white people because you're not one of them? Then there are rumors that you hate blacks as well. I don't want to be caught up in all that anymore. It's hard enough that people don't accept me for who I am."

"You've known me all these years and you are going to believe all those rumors over anything that I have to say?" Kendra asked. "You make it sound like I am prejudiced, but when those other people didn't like you because you were mixed, I didn't have a problem with your color then. It would make no sense for me to hate you now."

"Stop acting like I didn't also accept you because you are dark skinned," Marie snapped back. "I thought we were friends, but I can't be friends with someone who is sneaky and hates people. I didn't want to say anything, but I saw you and James holding hands that day, so what the other kids were saying must have some validity to it. You were just hiding your relationship with him. Maybe you only wanted to date him because you wanted status, his color, and not be black anymore. I don't know. None of what you are trying to do makes any sense to me."

"It makes no sense because none of it is true," said Kendra. "James is the one who wanted to date me. He is the one who was holding my hand. Just because you hold someone's hand doesn't mean that you are dating. If I held your hand, would it be fair to say that I am dating you?"

"I don't know what to think any longer, Kendra," Marie said. "I just don't think that we can be friends anymore. I'm sorry. I just can't deal with anymore of this. I'm resigning from the art club. I guess you can finally say that you got what you wanted, now you can be president. It's what you've always wanted, right? Now you can be the leader since you are so perfect at everything."

Kendra remained in the hallway dumbfounded. Her friend was not only abandoning the art club that they had worked hard to create and manage but was abandoning their friendship as well. She watched as her last friend walked away from her. She was not wanted nor liked by any of her peers. She was alone. She walked into the empty room that used to have the art club in it. The only people that were there were her and Ms. Montrell. She sat down near her teacher, took out her project, and began to work on it. Ms. Montrell said nothing about the missing students and sat down next to Kendra, offering pointers on the project. Kendra thanked the teacher and walked to her locker afterwards. In the locker, the card that she had made for the teacher fell to the ground. She had forgotten to give it to the teacher a long time ago when she got caught up with the pressures from her other classes and the drama. It had both her signature and the signatures of the former students written on it.

"What good is giving her this card now?" she thought. "If they really appreciated anything, they still would be there to support both her and me. So much for all that..." She balled up the card and tossed it into the trash. When Kendra returned home, her father had told her that he had talked to Mrs. Boudreaux. He said that he was going to move forward with seeing if his daughter could be transferred to another nearby school. He told her not to worry and to keep making sure that her grades did not slip. Kendra frowned. She had no other choice. All that she had now were her grades. She had no friends, no art club, or allies.

Chapter 11

"Ooh, look what the cat dragged in," someone said in homeroom once Kendra entered. She ignored the student and sat down. She opened a book, hoping to distract herself from the other students and their negativity.

"Yo, why is it so quiet in here?" another student asked.

"'Cause someone went to the principal," Jarika said, nodding Kendra's way. "They said if we keep messin' with her, we gonna get suspended."

"She might as well, she part of the family now," someone laughed. "She had to get them to protect her from us. She scared."

"What's going on?" asked the substitute teacher.

"Nothing," Jarika said.

"Y'all need to leave 'ole girl alone," said another student. "I don't blame James. She is better than Whitney. I can't stand her."

"Shut up, Darrell," said Dominique.

"Well, it's true," said Darrell. "Whitney has a bad attitude with everyone, and I don't see why James even dated her to begin with. He's never looked happy around her."

"He's always walking around with that angry look on his face too," Jarika added. "He creeps me out sometimes and did y'all see how he sometimes walks around slamming his fists into the lockers? He's got issues."

"Well, after dating Whitney, can you blame him?" said Darrell.

"James is nothing compared to Andy," Dominique added. "He is crazy and doesn't care, period. He burps, farts, and cusses out everyone. The only person he is scared of is James because he beat him up in the 10th grade."

The bell rang and the students began to walk to their next class. Kendra waited for the last student to leave the class before making her exit. Moving swiftly down the hall, she kept a close look out for any paper balls that could possibly come her way. So far, things had gotten calm, and she was able to move to her next class without incident.

In the art class, she worked quietly on her project. Luckily a few of the students who had been causing chaos were absent that day, including Derrick Johnson and Andy Pearson. Some students were absent due to some illness that had been spreading in the school. As she worked, Eric placed a piece of paper between them. He wrote a note and tapped at the paper for her to read it.

I'm sorry about my friends. They can be some real jerks sometimes.

Surprised that someone was now not trying to be mean to her, Kendra's heart began to feel a little at ease. She reached for her pencil and began to write back.

Thanks. I thought that everyone hated me. It's nice to know that not everyone is cruel at this school.

Eric smiled and continued to write.

Well, I don't hate you and I don't believe any of those rumors. Some of them are just downright dumb. It just shows how stupid most people at this school are.

Kendra looked at Eric. He was one of James' friends and was also friends with Derrick and Andy. She wondered if what he was writing were true about how he felt. So many people had walked out of her life and didn't want to be her friend anymore. So far, he had done nothing to offend her. He had always been polite. Kendra began to write again.

Thanks. You have no idea how much it means to me for someone to tell me that.

Kendra watched as Eric smiled at the note. She paused and then continued to write.

Are you sure that you want to go against what your friends are saying and doing? They don't really like me.

Eric began to write.

They are my friends, but I don't have to agree with everything that they say or do.

Eric winked and continued to work on his project. He took the paper and discarded it in a nearby trashcan. Kendra smiled, looking down at her paper. She began to feel a little hopeful that at least one person believed her, even though he was friends with some negative people. She was glad that the seat next to Eric was open and she was able to sit next to him out of all the people in the class.

During lunch, Kendra did not go to the cafeteria like she normally would. There was nobody to sit next to anymore, especially without the drama that was still circulating throughout the school. She was in one of the few safe places that she could go to: the girl's bathroom. Luckily, nobody else took notice of her new hiding space as she began to eat a sandwich that her mother had made her the night before. Right now, her only friends were the writings on the bathroom walls. She read the messages. Some were very obscene, but she did not care. They were nicer than the names or comments that she had to deal with in other parts of the school by her peers.

After eating her sandwich, she remained in the bathroom, waiting for lunch to be over.

Soon, she heard the door to the main door open and the steps of some students walking in. She tucked her feet above the bottom crack of her stall.

"Have any of you seen Kendra at lunch?" Jarika asked.

"No," said Dominique, "She is probably eating with her boyfriend."

"Nah, James was eating in the cafeteria without her," another girl said. "I heard that she is in another art class flirting with another white boy. Damn, she moves fast. Pretty soon, she's gonna be with every white boy in the school and be like that hoe, Jane Adams."

"That would be nasty," said Dominique. "I'm tired of her making all of the rest of us look bad. Now, these white kids are mad at her and calling her all these racist names. This one kid named Andy shouted out, "black booger" in the hallway and I almost went off on his ass, but then I saw that he was talking to her."

"Yeah, but won't it be only a matter of time until they start going after the rest of us because we are black?" asked the other girl.

"If they do, we are gonna kick all their asses," said Jarika. "If Andy ever calls me the same names that he's been calling Kendra, I will rip all that red hair out of his scalp with one pull."

"I don't even see why Kendra even bothered to report us to the principal," said Dominique. "As bad as those white folks are treating her, she won't report them, but gonna snitch on us. I told you she hated black people. She is such a sellout. Always kissing up to massa."

Soon, Kendra heard the door to the bathroom open again and heard the sound of footsteps. She cracked the door to the stall that she was in and noticed that the girls were gone. She closed the door to the stall and stared at the floor. She hated the school and the students even more than ever. She did not want to go to her next class. Her father had told her that he was

going to do something to help her and even talked
to the principal, but nothing was being resolved.
She waited in the bathroom. Soon, it was time to
go to her next class. Instead of going, she
remained in the bathroom, not caring that her
next tardy would mean that she would get a
detention that day.

Chapter 12

Kendra sat down in an unfamiliar desk. She had her first detention. She was sad to see Whitney in another desk a few rows away from her. Whitney didn't say anything as she was reapplying her makeup. There were two other students in the room with them. One was Darrell who just sat there leaning his chair in its back two legs, swaying back and forth. The other was another girl who was staring out the window. Everyone was silent. After what seemed like an eternity, detention was over. The teacher walked out the door. Whitney zipped her bag closed.

"Guess Ms. Goody Two Shoes couldn't get out of her detention," she said to Kendra. "Watch out, Pauline, she might try to steal your boyfriend too."

The other girl looked at Kendra with a questionable look.

"James shouldn't even like black girls," Whitney continued. "They are so ugly!"

"Wait a minute," Darrell intervened. "You need to shut up. If you were so hot, you wouldn't need to put on as much make up for the last 15 minutes. He doesn't even like you."

"If he didn't like me, we wouldn't be dating, duh," said Whitney.

"All he does is complain about you to the football team," the boy continued. "In fact, the whole school doesn't like you. The only person who likes you is Beth and even that is uncertain."

"Darrell, you aren't even seeing anyone, so you have no room to talk," said Whitney.

"I'd rather be single than date someone like you," Darrell said. "I'm tired of all you dumb racist people at the school. You only hate Kendra because James likes her more than you and you are only using her race as an excuse to hate her because there is nothing else to hate on. She looks better than you, is smarter than you, and even has your so called man's eye. Sounds like she is winning to me."

Angry, Whitney stormed out of the room. The rest of the three students walked out the room. The other girl walked one way and Darrell walked another. Kendra followed Darrell.

"Thanks," she said.

Darrell glanced at her momentarily and continued his walk. Kendra turned around and walked home, feeling a little more hopeful about some of the students at the school. She returned home to find her mother's car in the driveway and her mother sitting out on the porch. Her mother looked at her, concerned.

"I heard you got a detention today," she said.

"I did," said Kendra.

"Did you skip class again because of the bullying?" her mother asked.

"Yes, ma'am."

"I know that it's hard being at that school, but don't let all of that drama interfere with your success. Your father was able to get a fulltime job with another construction company on the other side of town. It seems to be a much better area than this one. We are going to be moving into that part of town and are working on transferring you to another school. Do not tell anyone. The less people know the better. We will all get to start over."

Kendra smiled. She was happy to learn that she would have the opportunity to have a better life somewhere else. She hoped that the students at her new school would be nicer than the Wood Oak High School students. She felt relieved. Things were starting to head in a more positive direction for not only her, but the rest of her family.

Chapter 13

During the next art class, most of the students were gagging. Andy had taken it upon himself to make a lot of belching and farting sounds during the class, grossing out most of the students. Ms. Montrell had already given him a detention for disturbing the class, but the behavior continued. When she would send him to the office to speak to the administrators, it would only be a matter of time until he would return to the class and not change his behavior. Finally, Eric turned around and spoke to his friend.

"Bro," he said. "That's enough. You're grossing everyone out. How much gas can you have?"

"Enough to mess around with Ms. Monty," Andy whispered.

"If you don't stop, Ms. Montrell could have Mrs. Gonzalez follow you around like she is doing with James. Would you like for that to happen?"

Immediately, the belching and farting stopped. The class was finally quiet again. Derrick was suspended for tossing paper at the teacher and getting caught. His chair was empty, but Andy began to use it as a tool to prop up his feet. With only ten minutes left of class, Ms. Montrell asked for volunteers to pick up the assignments. She called on both Andy and another student. Both students began to collect the papers. Kendra began to pack her belongings. As for now, things had gotten quieter at the school, with the exception of a few slurs here and there, but it was not as chaotic as before. Jarika and Monique had been more quiet than usual during homeroom and the other classes. Whitney was more vocal, but not as frequent with her insults since that day in detention. She would roll her eyes and hold her nose in the air at the sight of Kendra.

As usual, there were no other kids at the art club with the exception of Kendra. She still went to the classroom when she could after school. She had finally managed to center the clay more effectively and had begun to start trying to make cylinders with the clay. Since she was the only member, Ms. Montrell had begun teaching only her how to work with the clay. Kendra was learning more and appreciated the one-on-one time but wished that she was sharing that moment with some of her old friends. However, they had made their choice and she made hers.

While cleaning up after the wheel throwing, Kendra was surprised to see Ms. Montrell walk up to her with a puzzled look on her face.

"Kendra," she said, "are you still working on the last project? I was looking through everyone's papers and noticed that yours was missing. Did you forget to turn it in or are you still working on it?"

"No," said Kendra. "I turned it in today during class. My project was finished on time."

"I do not see it in the pile," Ms. Montrell said, going through the stack of papers again with Kendra. Her paper was missing. Kendra walked up to the area where the students usually kept their portfolios and looked in there. Her paper was not there. She looked at her teacher with sadness in her eyes.

"I don't know what happened to my paper," she said. "I do remember turning it in to Andy. I don't have it. I don't know where it could have gone. I'm sorry."

"It isn't like you to not turn in your paper," said Ms. Montrell. "You can take some time and try to find your paper or redo the assignment and turn it in at the end of the week."

"Yes, ma'am," Kendra said sadly. She sighed deeply as she picked up her bag. She walked out of the room and began her walk home, upset. She had spent a whole week working on her project and it was gone. Now, she would have to start over so that she could get a grade for the assignment. Redoing the assignment would mean that it would take time away from her other classes which she was still struggling to balance out her studying. Once she got home, she immediately began to work on her missing paper. She would have to push back her work in her other classes. If she would manage her time, she could still have time to do her homework in her other classes after working on her art project. It was 4 p.m. when she began to redo her assignment. The next time she glanced at the clock, it was 6 p.m.

"I'm so tired," Kendra thought.

"Kendra," her mother called out from another room, "are you coming down for dinner?"

"I can't," said Kendra. "I have an important assignment to work on and I need to keep working on it."

"I'll bring you a plate to your room," her mother said.

"I hate rushing to do assignments," Kendra muttered to herself. With her free hand, she began to grab strands of her hair and unwittingly began to pull the strands of her hair out. Her pencil quickly went from being sharp and pointed, to dull and down to the wood stump. She quickly sharpened her pencil and resumed doing her drawing.

There was a knock at the door and Mrs. Williams opened it. She placed the plate of food on the other side of Kendra's desk, looked at her daughter's drawing, and the strands of hair that had fallen to the side of the paper.

"Don't panic," her mother said. "Just calm down. Remember what we talked about."

"My paper is gone," Kendra said, wrapping her fingers around another strand of hair and pulling it out. Her mother grabbed her hand. Kendra looked down, finally noticing what she was doing. She looked down at the paper and saw the clumps of hair that was now on her paper. She paused.

"Just take a deep breath," Mrs. Williams said. "Calm down." She grabbed the bottle of perfume that was sitting on her daughter's dresser and sprayed it. The scent began to calm Kendra down. She slowly looked down at the hair. It had been a while since she had pulled her hair out. She only did that when her panic attacks would get worse. She had been trying to use aroma therapy for years. Her mother had gotten her a scent of perfume from the store to help her smell something nice to pull her daughter out of her severe anxiety and depression while attending school.

"I have to start over with my assignment," Kendra said, frowning. "I thought I turned my paper in, but the teacher and I couldn't find it, so now I have to redo it."

"How much time is she giving you?"

"Until the end of the week."

"Do you think you need more time than that?"

"If I ask for more time, then it will only push back another assignment in another class and I'm already behind. I just feel like a failure with too many demands from each of my classes. I don't want to disappoint you and dad if my grades get lower than A's. I am trying; I really am."

Mrs. Williams embraced her daughter.

"Your dad and I know that you are working hard. You don't have to be perfect in everything. You have never been a disappointment to us. If you need more time to complete the assignment, please tell your teacher. If you need for me to talk to her I will."

"I'll talk to her and ask for more time," Kendra said, feeling a little relieved.

"Why don't you take a break and eat your dinner," Mrs. Williams suggested. "Whatever you do not finish today, there is always tomorrow. Sometimes things happen beyond our control. She is going to give you extra time to redo the assignment, so you do not have to finish everything tonight in one sitting."

"Okay," Kendra said, smiling.

Chapter 14

The next day at school, Kendra received permission to go to the art classroom to work on her project during her homeroom period. Ms. Montrell even gave her an extension to complete to project by an additional week. Ms. Montrell's homeroom class was quiet and were not distracting like her fifth period class. Kendra wished that she was in that homeroom class. At least there were no bullies there. Once the bell rang, Kendra put her drawing into her portfolio and headed to her next class. Most of the day was uneventful. Jarika and Monique didn't bother Kendra other than the occasional eye roll. Whitney even ignored her. It was as if things were getting slowly better. Even James didn't say anything to her, but he would still have this longing look in his eyes as she would walk past him in the hallway.

Soon, it was time for the art class. As usual, Andy did his typical gross sounds in the back of the classroom, until Eric had to intervene.

"Dude," he said. "Enough already! Damn!"

"He is so disgusting!" a nearby student said.

"I wish that it was him that got suspended instead of Derrick," another student said.

"Shut up, before I flick another booger at you!" Andy shouted.

"Andy, you have another detention," Ms. Montrell said.

"So what, Ms. Monty," Andy said. "I already have one in another class. What's one more?"

Ms. Montrell called the office. Soon, Andy was called into the office. He kicked a chair as he walked out of the classroom.

"I'm so sick of students like him," someone groaned.

"He is freakin' nasty. Why won't he just drop out of school since he hates it so much?" another student said.

Kendra looked at Eric. He looked annoyed as well but kept working on his assignment. Most of the class continued their talks about how annoyed they were at Andy. Soon, he was back in the classroom, unfazed about going into the office. He sat back down in his chair and yawned.

"Yo," a kid named DJ Evans said to Andy, "they were talkin' shit about you while you were gone, bro."

"What they say this time?" Andy asked him.

"They said they were sick of you and that you needed to drop out of school," DJ said.

"Who said that?" Andy demanded.

"I dunno," DJ said. "It came from Kendra's direction."

"Really?" Andy said, looking at Kendra. "Why don't you say that to me in my face, bitch."

Kendra turned around, angry.

"I didn't say anything about you," she said.

"Don't be scared now," Andy said. "I'm back. If you're going to talk about me, say it now."

Eric turned around, looking at Andy.

"It wasn't her, bro," he said. "Just chill. Everyone talks crap at this school, you included. You don't even have any proof that she said anything. I'm sitting right next to her and I know it wasn't her."

"Stop trying to defend her," Andy said. "Just because James likes her doesn't mean that I'm going to kiss her ass like you are. She better watch her back, dumb bitch."

"Just shut up," Kendra snapped, throwing her pencil at him. "I didn't say anything about you. I'm sick of people like you blaming me for things that I didn't do or say. Leave me alone."

"Oooohhhh, she threw a pencil at you," DJ said to Andy. "You gonna let her do that and embarrass you like that, bro?"

"You shut up too," Kendra said to DJ. "All you do is be messy and try to start drama. Are you sure that you are even a boy with all the mess that comes out of your mouth?"

Some of the students began to snicker. DJ and Andy remained silent and glared at Kendra with anger. Soon they began to whisper amongst themselves. Eric's pencil fell to the floor. Kendra grabbed it and handed it back to him.

"Here's your pencil," she said.

"T-thanks," Eric said.

It was now time to collect the papers. Andy began to collect the papers for his section of the class. Before he could grab Kendra's, Eric grabbed it.

"I'll turn it in, dude," he said.

Andy placed the papers on Ms. Montrell's desk, walked back to where DJ was sitting, and continued to whisper to him. Soon, both boys walked out of the classroom.

Kendra watched as Eric placed both her paper and his paper on the teacher's desk. She was happy that he had collected her paper and not Andy. She was also glad to finally stand up to some of the students who were bullying her or spreading lies about her. Enough was enough. She felt proud of herself. She had found her voice. She grabbed her bag and walked to her locker. As she opened the locker, she felt a tight squeeze on her buttocks. Immediately, she turned around and saw Andy grinning at her. She slapped him, dropping her books. Students began to freeze in the hallway.

"Did you guys see that?" someone in the crowd asked.

"She totally slapped him!"

"Why'd she slap Andy?"

"I dunno. She just slapped him for no reason!"

Bursting into tears, Kendra ran as fast as she could to the office. She no longer cared about her classes or school. She hated school and everyone in it. She had finally had enough. She opened the office door and ran to the counselor's office. She punched the door with all her might. The door flew open, revealing the counselor with another student who was looking confused.

"Oh, my goodness," said Mrs. Gonzalez. She closed the door behind her, leaving the other student alone. She walked Kendra to the principal's office. Mrs. Boudreaux looked surprised to see them and closed the door behind them.

Chapter 15

Kendra stared at the ceiling to her room, her tears long dried out. Her hair pulled once again. She turned away from the books that were gathered on her desk. Her mother had picked her up earlier that day and brought her home. Kendra had gone to both the counselor and principal about the event that had occurred in the hallway. They said that they would be investigating the incident, angering her parents.

"We are going to keep her home for the next few days," her mother said in the office that day. She didn't blame her daughter and told her to rest and to talk to her once she was ready. Kendra only wanted to be alone. She didn't want anything from anybody anymore. She trusted nobody. She stayed in her bed in a fetal position, in the dark. Soon, there was a knock at the door. It was her mother.

"We still have a few more days until you are officially transferred to the other school," she said. "After everything you've been through, we are also going to make sure that you see a counselor, thanks to your dad's new insurance. It kicks in a few days. Your dad is still trying to secure the new apartment for us. I've gathered your belongings from the school. If you don't do any of the work, I don't blame you. The school knows about the situation and said that they will be suspending the student...I hate to say this, but the school also informed me that there was a video made of you slapping the student in the hallway that is being circulated online. The boy's parents are saying that you are at fault for hitting their son and the school suspended you as well, unfortunately. They changed the boy's schedule, but it doesn't matter, we are still pulling you out of that horrible school."

"Why would there be a video?" Kendra asked. "What if the other school or universities ever find out about it? Won't I get in trouble, and it ruin my future?"

"The school said that they are working on getting the video taken down, but it's not guarantee that things won't still circulate," her mother sighed. "Whatever you do, don't contact anyone from that school from this moment on.

We are still trying to get things set in place for you."

"Thanks," Kendra said, pulling up the covers to her chin.

Mrs. Williams frowned and walked out the room.

Chapter 16

Kendra sat down at her desk. She did not have to go to school that day. It was strange to wake up and not be there in the hallways sitting with the Rainbows, but then again, they had long left her. No longer would she have to be in the classroom with the bullies or the messy people who had made her life miserable. She felt her phone vibrate. To her surprise, it was James.

> **James:** I heard about what happened and I kicked Andy and DJ's asses. I didn't know that any of this was going to happen. I'm sorry that any of this happened. I heard that you were suspended for two weeks. I still want to keep in touch until you return to school.

> "No," Kendra thought. "I do not want to keep in touch. I don't want to have anything to do with that school any longer. I've done everything that I could to be a good student and peer and that was not enough. I want to move on and be in a better place where people are supportive and won't hurt me any longer."

She deleted his message and decided to never contact him again. She logged onto her social media account and found a friendship request from James as well. She declined it. She deleted most of the students from the school from her friend's list.

"Friendship does not hurt," she said, deleting more people. "Friendship does not abandon you when you are at your lowest point. If you cannot be there for me, what are you then?"

Once again, she felt her phone vibrate. She received a message from Marie.

Marie: I heard about what happened. I'm sorry. Message me back. I would like to talk to you.

Kendra thought about ignoring Marie's message as well, but deep down, something inside of her wanted to talk to her former friend, longing for the times before all the chaos erupted that severed their friendship. However, another part of Kendra was upset that she had been abandoned to begin with and questioned if Marie

126 | When They Bully: Rainbow Girl

and her even had a friendship that was beyond repair at that point.

Kendra: There is nothing more to talk about.

Marie: What do you mean? People are saying that both you and Andy were suspended and that there is a video of you slapping him.

Kendra: You seem to care a lot about what other people say, as usual.

Marie: I'm only telling you about what is going on at the school.

Kendra: I don't care about what is going on at the school anymore.

Marie: Well, I just wanted to say that I am sorry about how things went between us earlier. I thought about what you said, and I would like to be friends again. I would like to get the art club started again. You can be president.

Kendra: Sorry, but some things you cannot just start over with.

Marie: I've already started talking to some of the other students and they miss going there. We would like it if you would be there too.

Kendra: If any of you ever cared about me or the art club, you never would have left to begin with. If you are going to start over, it will be without me.

Marie: Why do you have to be like that? We've known each other for years. Can't you just forgive and forget that any of this ever happened?

Kendra: I've been through too much to forgive and forget that any of this ever happened. While it wasn't all you and the people from the art club solely, I was abandoned when I needed all of you the most and I'm moving on. Remember that you were the one who threw our friendship away first, not me.

Marie: I don't have time for this. I have to go. Text me back later, when you're not angry.

Kendra looked at her phone, angry. She felt that Marie and the people from school had a lot of nerve asking for her to continue to serve them as an official of the art club after they had abandoned both her and the club. She felt that none of the students deserved any more time of her time or energy. She walked out of her room and saw her mother sitting in the kitchen with a cup of coffee in her hands.

"Mom," Kendra said. "What's the name of the new school that I will be transferred to?"

"Lagniappe High School," Mrs. Williams said. "It's not that far from the new apartment. I did some research on it and it seems to be a pretty good school from what I've read. Maybe you can look up some information yourself about the different programs that they have. It seems to be pretty impressive. They have a good high school nursing program."

"Wasn't grandma a nurse?" asked Kendra.

"She was a licensed practical nurse," said Mrs. Williams. "She's long retired from it. Your dad said that she was a pretty good nurse. I'm sure that she can always answer your questions if you decide to go into nursing."

"But what if the people from the new school are just as bad as the ones from Wood Oak?"

"At this point, no school is worse than Wood Oak. You are absolutely not going back there. Get that school off of your mind and look forward from this point on. In three days, you will be a Lagniappe Lion."

Kendra smiled and walked back to her room. She turned on her computer and looked up the clubs from the new school that she would be transferring to. She scanned down the list of clubs and found out that they had their own art club. She looked at the pictures of the work done by the different students and looked at how proud they were to display their work. A smile slowly crossed her face. She continued to look up other activities and clubs offered by the school. It looked like a more diverse school. She hoped that she would be accepted by them and not hated due to her skin color, academics, and so forth. She found that the art club had a group on social media and sent a request to join. Additionally, she looked up the school's nursing program that her mother had mentioned, out of curiosity. She found a social media link from the school's account about the program. Kendra studied the pictures. The students were smiling and showed themselves with different equipment. She never thought that high schools had nursing programs, but her new school did. She clicked a request to join. Soon, there was a message that she had been accepted.

"They want me?" she thought, her eyes filling with tears. "They accepted me..."

She looked at the message boards with students sharing information about the classes. The students seemed to be supportive of one another. Nobody was arguing or talked bad about anyone. She swallowed hard and began to type a message.

Hi. I'm Kendra. I'm going to be joining the school soon.

She waited. Soon, there were messages.

Amyra: Welcome to the group, Kendra!

Stacey: Hi, Kendra! I can't wait to meet you!

Lyndsay: Hey, Kendra!

Frederick: Kendra! What's up?!

Floyd: Welcome Kendra!

More and more messages from students began to flood Kendra's post. Kendra began to cry, finally feeling accepted. She smiled as she began responding to their posts, looking forward to attending a new school and a new beginning.

Chapter 17

"Kendra," Mrs. Williams called out, "Make sure that you are labeling your boxes so that you know what's in them."

"Yes, ma'am," Kendra said, writing on the last box. Everything was packed and she was ready to go. The only thing that was left unpacked by her was a card that she had made the night before. She knew that she would not be able to give it to her teacher and asked for her mother to deliver it for her.

"Are you sure that you want me to do this?" Ms. Williams asked.

"I'm sure," said Kendra. "If I had to leave anything behind this would be it. Let me look over it first before you deliver it." Kendra scanned the written note to her card and handed it to her mother.

Ms. Montrell,

Thank you for all that you have done as a teacher. I really enjoyed your class and appreciate the extra time you spent after school

to ensure that the art club was a success. I learned how to draw, sculpt, and wheel throw. I never could have learned as much without your help, and I am grateful to have been your student. I am sorry for all of the horrible things that some of the students have done to you, but I stayed for as long as I could. You stayed for me too and never missed a day after school. Thanks for being there when nobody else was. Even though I will be attending another school, I wanted to say that I will never forget you. I hope that, in the future when I am stronger, I can serve as a positive role model for others and be there for them in my own way as you have done for me.

Kendra